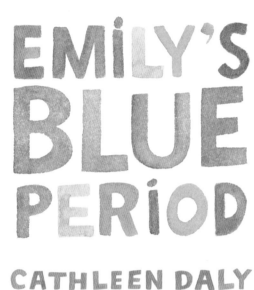

EMILY'S BLUE PERIOD

CATHLEEN DALY

ILLUSTRATIONS BY LISA BROWN

A NEAL PORTER BOOK
ROARING BROOK PRESS
NEW YORK

Text copyright © 2014 by Cathleen Daly
Illustrations copyright © 2014 by Lisa Brown
A Neal Porter Book
Published by Roaring Brook Press
Roaring Brook Press is a division of Holtzbrinck Publishing Holdings Limited Partnership
175 Fifth Avenue, New York, New York 10010

The art for this book was created using pencil and watercolor on paper, with some digital collage.
mackids.com

Library of Congress Cataloging-in-Publication Data
Daly, Cathleen.
    Emily's blue period / Cathleen Daly ; illustrated by Lisa Brown. --
First edition.
        pages cm
    "A Neal Porter Book."
    Summary: After her parents get divorced, Emily finds comfort in making
and learning about art.
    ISBN 978-1-59643-469-1
    [1. Art—Fiction. 2. Divorce—Fiction.] I. Brown, Lisa, 1972-
illustrator. II. Title.
    PZ7.D16945Em 2014
    [E]—dc23
                                                                    2013016727

Roaring Brook Press books may be purchased for business or promotional use. For information
on bulk purchases please contact Macmillan Corporate and Premium Sales Department at
(800) 221-7945 x5442 or by email at specialmarkets@macmillan.com.

First edition 2014
Printed in China by Toppan Leefung Printing Ltd., Dongguan City, Guangdong Province

1   3   5   7   9   10   8   6   4   2

CONTENTS

This book is dedicated to my family.
—C.D.

To my picture book family: Ashley, Christy, Julie, and Katherine
—L.B.

CHAPTER ONE

Emily wants to be an

In school Emily is learning about
a famous artist named Pablo Picasso.

His full name was

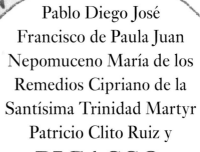

Pablo Diego José Francisco de Paula Juan Nepomuceno María de los Remedios Cipriano de la Santísima Trinidad Martyr Patricio Clito Ruiz y

PICASSO.

7

Emily's name is
EMILY ROSE PINCHNER.
She wants to change it to

EMILY EMILIA ROSITA JENNY JUANITA de los ALTO IGOR de la EYEBALL MONTOYA FLUFFY → PINCHNER

So far her parents won't let her.

Picasso was a cubist.

Sometimes he broke his pictures up into cubes and unusual shapes. Things in his paintings weren't where you'd expect them to be.

He may scoot a nose way over, putting it far away from where it usually goes.

Or stack an eye right on top of another eye!

He liked to mix things up.

9

So does Emily.

CHAPTER TWO

AX LEM~~ED~~IPU
ALL MIXED UP

Lately, Emily's family is mixed up.
She doesn't like this.

Emily's dad is no longer
where he belongs.

DAD

Suddenly, he
lives in his own
little cube.

STOP

13

Dad needs to pick out furniture for his new home.

Emily sees little cubes everywhere.

STUF

IN

"Do you like this?" asks Dad. It's a
soft cube you can put your feet on.

"What about this?"
It's a big square rug.

No.

Everything is pretty, but nothing looks like home.

"WHERE'S JACK?" says Dad a moment later.

Jack is hiding behind a big couch. He won't come out.

This is my
FORTRESS!
No one can come back here!

"Come on, Jack," says Dad.
But Jack won't budge.

He stares at the other busy shoppers. Emily watches, too. Jack is quiet. Dad reaches back and scratches Jack's head.

BIG MISTAKE.

THIS IS MY COUCH FORTRESS AND NO ONE CAN TOUCH ME! NO ARMS ALLOWED IN MY FORTRESS!

Now the shoppers are staring at Dad and Emily.

ALL RIGHT, ENOUGH!

Dad picks up Jack like a sack of potatoes. They leave the big square store without a thing for Dad's new apartment. Just a silent bag of potatoes that looks like a boy.

CHAPTER THREE

BLUE

That week Emily's teacher calls her mom.

Then why didn't you do your project?

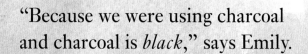

"Because we were using charcoal
and charcoal is *black*," says Emily.

"What's wrong with black?"

SIGH.
I can't use black
because I am in
my blue period.

"When Pablo Picasso was very sad
he only painted in shades of blue.
And now I am in *my* blue period."

It is a little early
in my career to be
having a blue period,
but it is happening
all the same.

33

Emily nuzzles her head into the
spot under her mother's arm where
it fits just like a puzzle piece.

Emily's Blue Period lasts quite some time.

CHAPTER FOUR

COLLAGE

One day, Emily learns about collage in art class.

It's a kind of artwork Picasso and his friend Braque liked to use. You add all kinds of things together to make a piece of art.

Emily can't wait to try.

37

Okay, class. I want you to make a collage of your house. You can use anything on this table that reminds you of home.

Emily sits very still. She has two homes. Which one should she make?

She sits and stares at her blank paper for the rest of the class.

40

Well, you can't really have
two homes can you?

"Why not?" asks Mom. "A lot of people
have more than one home."

Home is where the heart
is. That's what it says on
Billy's mom's potholder.

Emily is quiet all through the rest of dinner. She moves all the different kinds of food on her plate into the shape of a heart before she eats it.

43

After dinner Emily starts digging through things.

The recycling.

Her mother's sewing kit.

The junk drawer.

Like a little animal burrowing here and there. Stashing things away into a little brown bag.

That Saturday she burrows into
things at her dad's apartment, too.

The wet bar.

The toolbox.

The top desk drawer.
Then she gets to work.

45

And work and work.

Cutting and gluing, gluing and cutting some more.

CHAPTER FIVE

BIG and SOGGY and Beautiful

Finally she is done. It's big and soggy
and beautiful. Back at Mom's, Emily
hangs the collage up to dry.

48

"Yep," says Emily. "I mostly make collages now. That's a collage of my home."

"Well, it's not a house, but it's my *home*. It's the home of my heart," says Emily. "See all the stuff from Dad's *and* Mom's plus Jack's head cut out of a photo and Jenny's friendship bracelet and other stuff that shows what's important to me."

Emily, I love your collage.

I'm glad my head is important to you, Em.

51

Right before bed, Emily notices
a purple blob in the middle
of her collage.

MOM!
Jack scribbled
on my collage!

Mom and Jack come running.

I DIDN'T!
I DIDN'T!

"It's not a scribble! It's a purple *heart*," says Jack. "I think your collage is the home of my heart, too!"

I'm sorry.

OH.

Emily is remembering what her teacher said about collage.
How you take things from different places to make a whole.

"Really?" says Jack.
"You mean it?"

"Really," says Emily.

And she does.

Now her collage is

PERFECT.